A PLACE CALLED
FREEDOM

A PLACE CALLED
FREEDOM

by
Scott Russell Sanders
illustrated by Thomas B. Allen

ATHENEUM BOOKS FOR YOUNG READERS

For Jessie, Sarah, Lauren, and Mark
–S. R. S.

For my friend, Tom Feelings
–T. B. A.

Atheneum Books for Young Readers
An imprint of Simon & Schuster Children's Publishing Division
1230 Avenue of the Americas
New York, New York 10020

Text copyright © 1997 by Scott Russell Sanders
Illustrations copyright © 1997 by Thomas B. Allen

Book design by Becky Terhune
The text of this book is set in Aunt Mildred.
The illustrations are rendered in pastels.

Printed in the United States of America
First Edition

10 9 8 7 6 5 4 3 2 1

Library of Congress Cataloging-in-Publication Data
Sanders, Scott R. (Scott Russell).
A place called Freedom / by Scott Russell Sanders ;
illustrated by Thomas B. Allen.—1st ed.
p. cm.
Summary: After being set free from slavery in 1832, young
James Starman and his family journey from Tennessee to Indiana
to start a new life and over the years they are joined by so many
blacks that they start their own town.
ISBN 0-689-80470-9
1. Afro-Americans—History—1815–1861—Juvenile Fiction.
[1. Afro-Americans—History—1815–1861—Fiction. 2. Frontier and
pioneer life—Indiana—Fiction. 3. Family life—Fiction. 4. Indiana—Fiction.]
I. Allen, Thomas B., ill. II. Title.
PZ7.S19786P 1997
[E]—dc20 95-52368

Down in Tennessee, on the plantation where I was born, Mama worked in the big house and Papa worked in the fields. The master of that big house set us free in the spring of 1832, when I was seven years old and my sister, Lettie, was five.

Papa called Lettie a short drink of water, because she was little and wriggly, and he called me a long gulp of air, because I was tall and full of talk.

As soon as we could pack some food and clothes, we left the plantation, heading north for Indiana. Our aunts and uncles and cousins who were still slaves hugged us hard and waved until we were out of sight.

Papa said it would be safer to travel at night.

"How're we going to find our way in the dark?" I asked him.

"We'll follow the drinking gourd," Papa answered. He pointed to the glittery sky, and I saw he meant the Big Dipper. He showed me how to find the North Star by drawing an arrow from the dipper's lip. Papa loved stars. That's why, when he gave up his old slave's name and chose a new one, he called himself Joshua Starman. And that's why my name is James Starman.

It was a weary, long way. Night after night as we traveled, the buttery bowl of the moon filled up, then emptied again. When Lettie got tired, she rode on Papa's shoulders for a while, or on Mama's hip. But I walked the whole way on my own feet.

At last one morning, just after sunrise, we came to the Ohio River. A fisherman with a face as wrinkled as an old boot carried us over the water in his boat. On the far shore we set our feet on the free soil of Indiana. White flowers covered the hills that day like feathers on a goose.

By and by we met a Quaker family who took us into their house, gave us seed, and loaned us a mule and a plow, all because they believed that slavery was a sin. We helped on their farm, working shoulder to shoulder, and we planted our own crops.

That first year Papa raised enough corn and wheat for us to buy some land beside the Wabash River, where the dirt was as black as my skin. Papa could grow anything, he could handle horses, and he could build a barn or a bed.

Before winter, Papa and Mama built us a sturdy cabin. Every night we sat by the fire and Papa told stories that made the shadows dance. Every morning Mama held school for Lettie and me. Mama knew how to read and write from helping with lessons for the master's children. She could sew clothes that fit you like the wind, and her cooking made your tongue glad.

While the ground was still frozen, Papa rode south through the cold nights, down to the plantation in Tennessee. We fretted until he showed up again at our door, leading two of my aunts, two uncles, and five cousins. They stayed with us until they could buy land near ours and build their own cabins.

Again and again Papa went back to Tennessee, and each time he came home with more of the folks we loved.

Hearing about our settlement, black people arrived from all over the South, some of them freed like us, some of them runaways. There were carpenters and black-smiths, basket weavers and barrel makers.

Soon we had a church, then a store, then a stable, then a mill to grind our grain. For the first time in our lives, we had money, just enough to get by, and we watched every penny.

After a few years, the railroad decided to run tracks through our village, because so many people had gathered here. If our place was going to be on the map, it needed a name. At a meeting, folks said we should call it Starman, in honor of Mama and Papa. But Mama and Papa said, "No, let's name it Freedom."

And that's how we came to live in a place called Freedom.

We all celebrated the new name by building a school, where Mama could teach everyone, young and old, to read and write and do sums. She made me want to learn everything there was to know.

When Mama first told me about the alphabet, I wondered how I could ever remember twenty-six different letters. But I learned them all in a flash. It was like magic to me, the way those letters joined up to make words.

Papa's farming was also like magic. He would put seeds in the ground, and before you knew it, here came melon vines or cornstalks. He planted trees, and here came apples or nuts or shade.

For a long while, I couldn't decide whether I wanted to grow up and become a farmer like Papa or a teacher like Mama.

"I don't see why a teacher can't farm," Mama said.

"I don't see why a farmer can't teach," said Papa.

They were right, you know, because I raised the beans and potatoes for supper, and I wrote these words with my own hand.